Disney
ONCE UPON A SNOWMAN

Adapted by **Suzanne Francis**

Illustrated by the **Disney Storybook Art Team**

A Random House PICTUREBACK® Book

Random House 🏠 New York

rhcbooks.com
ISBN 978-0-7364-4157-5
Printed in the United States of America
10 9 8 7 6 5 4 3 2 1

High upon the snow-covered North Mountain, Elsa, Queen of Arendelle, let her power over snow and ice fly from her fingers. She created **swirling patterns of ice** with her magic.

With another gentle wave of her hand, something else appeared . . . **a snowman**!

The snowman stood still, as snowmen tend to do. He had two twig arms, three coal buttons, and a **big smile**.

Elsa walked farther up the North Mountain, tossing her cape into the wind.

She didn't notice when her **cape** landed right on the snowman!

The little snowman tumbled blindly
down the mountainside.

"**Oof! Ow! What's happening?**" he cried. "I appear to be some sort of snowman. **How absurd!**"

The snowman wandered into the forest.
"Hello?" he called. "Anybody there?
I'm having a bit of a **crisis of identity**!"
No one answered.

The little snowman
walked and walked through
the quiet, snowy woods
until **night** fell.

He was thrilled to finally come upon signs of life. He'd found **Wandering Oaken's Trading Post and Sauna**!

"Hoo-hoo!" sang Oaken, the shopkeeper, as the bell on the door jingled. He paused briefly when he saw that his new customer was a **snowman**. Then he asked the guest what he needed.

They tried lots
of noses on Olaf,
including a **flag** . . .

When the snowman noticed
he didn't have a nose, he asked
if Oaken had any **carrots**—and
Oaken told him he had just sold
the last of them.

"But I'm sure I can find you
something that will fit the bill!"
he said.

a **fish** that smelled
pretty stinky . . .

and even a **snow globe**!

Nothing seemed quite right.

The snowman picked up a stereoscope and looked through it. Something inside him went POP-BANG-ZOOM!

"What is *this*?" he asked, mesmerized by the pictures he saw.

"That would be SUMMER," answered Oaken.

The snowman watched wide-eyed as Oaken shuffled through the summer scenes. He wanted to know everything about summer, and believed it was the **perfect place** for a snowman like him!

That gave Oaken an idea.

Oaken found a nice *summer* sausage for the snowman to wear
for a nose. The snowman thanked him, then headed for the door.

"I'm off to find my name!" he said as he tromped back toward the woods. **"Ah! What a nose!"** *Sniiiffff!* **"Processed meat!"**

It wasn't long before a **pack of wolves** caught the scent of the snowman's sausage nose. They began to chase him.

The snowman's **twig arms** fell beneath his feet. He sped away on them as if they were skis!

He raced down the mountain, **barely escaping** the wolves! In all the chaos, the sausage broke.

The snowman safely landed on a ledge. But he heard a **scratching sound**—one of the wolves was trying to get to him!

The snowman backed up against the rocky mountain wall. Unable to reach the snowman's sausage nose, the wolf **whimpered and whined**. It looked very sad. And very **hungry**.

The snowman sighed. "**You** need this even more than I do," he said. He tossed the sausage to the wolf, who ate it happily.

Then the snowman slipped and fell! But the wolf simply licked his face, showering him with kisses before taking off.

"That felt just like a warm hug," he said.

And suddenly, a **memory** came to him of two girls, and he recalled something very important.

"I'm Olaf," he said. **"And I like warm hugs."**

Bursting with joy, Olaf continued along the mountain. He gasped when he spotted some people and a reindeer walking below. He quickly headed down the slope to meet them.

A familiar voice said, **"Who knew winter could be so beautiful?"** Olaf picked up his pace, eager to introduce himself.